P9-DVM-695

For Larry Dobrow and Benjamin Dobrow,
my tightest of knits without whom
I'd lose my wits—A. T.

LITTLE SIMON
An imprint of Simon & Schuster Children's Publishing Division
1230 Avenue of the Americas, New York, New York 10020
Copyright © 2013 by Simon & Schuster, Inc.
All rights reserved, including the right of reproduction in whole or in part in any form.
LITTLE SIMON is a registered trademark of Simon & Schuster, Inc.,
and associated colophon is a trademark of Simon & Schuster, Inc.
For information about special discounts for bulk purchases, please contact
Simon & Schuster Special Sales at 1-866-506-1949 or business@simonandschuster.com.
The Simon & Schuster Speakers Bureau can bring authors to your live event.
For more information or to book an event contact the Simon & Schuster Speakers Bureau
at 1-866-248-3049 or visit our website at www.simonspeakers.com.
Designed by Laura DiSiena and Laura Roode
Photographs by Michael Frost
Characters constructed by Erika Burling
Manufactured in China 0613 SCP
First Edition
2 4 6 8 10 9 7 5 3 1
Library of Congress Cataloging-in-Publication Data
Tabby, Abigail, author. Meet the KnitWits! / by Abigail Tabby.
pages cm Summary: After moving to their new house, the literal-minded KnitWits
host a housewarming party by wrapping blankets around the chimney,
serving drinks using a racket, and icing the cake in the freezer.
ISBN 978-1-4424-5342-5 (hardcover : alk. paper)
[1. Moving, Household—Fiction. 2. Family life—Fiction. 3. Humorous
stories.] I. Title. PZ7.T1124Me 2013 [E]—dc23
2012040111
ISBN 978-1-4424-5343-2 (eBook)

the Knitwits
MAKE a MOVE!

by
ABIGAIL TABBY

illustrated by
LEE WILDISH

characters constructed by
ERIKA BURLING

LITTLE SIMON

New York   London   Toronto   Sydney   New Delhi

The KnitWits were moving into their new house!

"Are you ready to move?" asked Mr. KnitWit.
"We sure are!" said Big KnitWit.
"Ready, set . . . **move!**" cried Mrs. KnitWit.
And all the KnitWits began to wiggle.

"Keep on moving!" called
Mr. KnitWit as he led the way.

The KnitWits moved all the way to their new home.
"Oh, my," said Mrs. KnitWit when they arrived.
"There sure is a lot to do.
Okay, KnitWits. Let's start
unpacking!"

So the KnitWits unpacked as
fast as they could.
"Done!" called
Little KnitWit.

"Now what?" asked Big KnitWit.
"We should have a **housewarming** party!"
said Mrs. KnitWit.
"Splendid!" replied Mr. KnitWit.
"Let's warm the house!"

So the KnitWits pulled all the scarves and sweaters that they could to warm the house inside and out. "It feels nice and warm to me!" said Little KnitWit.

"We should have some snacks ready
for our new neighbors," said Mr. KnitWit.
"Excellent idea!" said Mrs. KnitWit.
"What shall we **serve?**"

"Something sweet!" said Little KnitWit.
"Something salty!" said Big KnitWit.
"We can serve both!" said Mrs. KnitWit.

"My serve is a little rusty," warned
Mrs. KnitWit, "so watch out."
Mrs. KnitWit held up the snacks, grabbed
her racket, and swung.

"Great serve!" said Mr. KnitWit.
Big KnitWit and Little KnitWit clapped.
Baby KnitWit ducked.

"You know what would be *really* special?" asked
Mr. KnitWit. "A cake to celebrate the new house!"
"That would be delicious!" said Mrs. KnitWit.
"Let's bake one!"
So the KnitWits helped Mrs. KnitWit bake a cake.

Mrs. KnitWit looked at the cake. "It could use a
bit of **icing**," she said. "Come on, KnitWits!
Let's ice this cake!"
So they carried the cake to the freezer.
It *just* fit.

"That should be nice and iced soon!" said Mrs. KnitWit.

"You know," said Mrs. KnitWit, looking around, "if we're having company we should really **straighten up**."
"Does this look straight now?" asked Big KnitWit, straightening out a picture.
"Oh, that looks lovely," said Mrs. KnitWit.

"Let's straighten everything!" said
Mr. KnitWit.
So the KnitWits straightened up
everything they could.

"I think we're ready for the party to begin,"
said Mrs. KnitWit.
"Let's **throw open the door** then!" said Mr. KnitWit.
All the KnitWits gathered round and counted,
"One, two, two and a half . . . three!"
Then they threw open the door.

"Come in, neighbors!" said the KnitWits.
"Welcome to our new home!"
Everyone came in to see how
the KnitWits had settled in.

Mrs. KnitWit continued to serve snacks.
And Mr. KnitWit cut the iced cake.
All the neighbors welcomed the KnitWits
to the neighborhood.

After everyone left, the KnitWits relaxed.
"What a wonderful party," said Big KnitWit.
"Everyone warmed our house just right,"
said Mrs. KnitWit. "It's **toasty**."

"And cozy," added Little KnitWit.
"It's perfect," said Mr. KnitWit.

Soon they were all ready for bed.
"**Sleep tight**, KnitWits," Mrs. KnitWit called.
So everyone snuggled in as close and tight as they could.
Because the KnitWits are a tightly knit bunch.

BED TIME